Selma

Aunt Rachel

Big David

The Blumenthal twins

David the Blacksmith

Davy

Jacob

Jolly Aaron

Josef the Tailor

Benjamin

Deborah

Dedicated to everyone,
and everyone else.
M.M.

Me

Pa

Rivka

Isaak the
Cobbler

The publication of this book was supported
by the Lithuanian Culture Institute.

Translated from the Lithuanian
Akmenėlis by Jūra Avižienis

First published in the United Kingdom
in 2023 by Thames & Hudson Ltd,
181A High Holborn, London WC1V 7QX

First published in the United States of
America in 2023 by Thames & Hudson Inc.,
500 Fifth Avenue, New York, New York 10110

Original edition © 2020 Tikra knyga, Vilnius
Text © Marius Marcinkevičius
Illustrations © Inga Dagilė
This edition © 2023 Thames & Hudson Ltd,
London

British Library Cataloguing-in-Publication
Data. A catalogue record for this book is
available from the British Library

Library of Congress Control Number
2022947827

ISBN 978-0-500-65326-5

Printed in Latvia

MIX
Paper | Supporting
responsible forestry
FSC® C002795

Be the first to know about our new
releases, exclusive content and
author events by visiting
thamesandhudson.com
thamesandhudsonusa.com
thamesandhudson.com.au

the **PEBBLE**

An Allegory of the Holocaust

Written by
Marius Marcinkevičius

Illustrated by
Inga Dagilė

Translated by
Jūra Avižienis

Summer 1943

The kite shot up into the air, straight into
the sun. My eyes followed it.

"I wish I could fly away, past the gates.
To freedom," I whispered as I tightened
my grip on the string.

"Freedom's not on the other side of the gates,
but in here, in your heart," Rivka said. She
pressed her small, but strong, hand to my chest.

I could feel my heart pounding,

thump,

thump,

thump,

as if it was beating in time with the faint
sound coming from my friend's heart.
I felt the warmth of her hand and the
last rays of the summer sun on my face,
and I was happy.

My best friend Rivka
and I were up on the
roof and the whole
world was at our feet.

Below us, I could hear children
laughing, dogs barking, and
women chatting.

A gust of wind caught my kite.
The string snapped and it soared
above the red roofs.

But that was all right.

Let it fly!

Autumn was coming
and the wind would soon
bring colorful leaves.

We got down from the roof. I was a little bit afraid of being left alone up there.

I was afraid of the dark, too.

I was also afraid that Papa might not come back. But as long as Rivka was with me, I felt much braver.

Rivka was the bravest girl in the whole world. She even had a scar above her lip, which she was very proud of.

Back on solid ground, Rivka ran home
while I waited for her on the bench.

There was a bagel sitting next to me.
I couldn't wait to taste it. They were
rare here these days. So delicious,
so tempting … But I was waiting
patiently to share it with my friend.

I closed my eyes, daydreaming.
When I opened them, next to
me on the bench, a big black bird
with beady eyes was watching me.

Those black birds ... They arrived last spring
with the bees and the warm breezes—

big black

birds.

They were everywhere, watching us with their sharp eyes. Then came the men in black uniforms. And just like the birds, they scuttled around, cawing with that strange, raspy language of theirs.

Soon they built a wall and closed the gates.
We weren't allowed to leave. Those who did leave
never came back. Papa left too. He said that he
was going to work with the other men and would
come home soon.

But he didn't come home.

Nobody ever came home.

Sometimes it was only men who passed through the gates, but sometimes it was whole families. People with dead eyes would come to the empty houses. They had eyes like the fish my Aunt Celia used to sell in her shop—pale, coated with a light film, the film of death. Their skin was slimy and cold.

The people with the dead eyes would move through the empty homes, packing up everything that was left behind. They worked in silence. They couldn't speak because their mouths were full of water and their hearts did not beat. I think they were dead.

As they worked, a hundred silent eyes watched them.

The big black bird snatched up my bagel and flew away.

He was greedy. The bagel was much too big for him. It slipped out of his beak and fell into the yard. I moved towards it. I still had a chance to rescue it, but I wasn't fast enough. Shrieking, the bird plummeted down.

All of a sudden, a little dog shot out from a nearby stairwell, barking fiercely. His bark was tiny and shrill, but he came at the bird with determination. The bird dug his claws into the bagel, screamed, and pecked the little dog in the eye. He began to bleed.

I ran over and scooped the little dog into
my arms. He was trembling and whimpering.

I was trembling too.

I was scared.

And a bit embarrassed.

This little creature was braver
than me. And he didn't even
have a name. But I did.

My name is Eitan. My grandmother told me
that my name means "strong." So I must be
strong. Strong as steel. Like a rock. But right
then, I was scared. The bird was watching me
as I held the little dog close. Rivka flew out of
the stairwell and pulled the dog from my arms.

"You, you…"
she said. And without
finishing, she ran home.

The black bird croaked in
triumph and flapped away,
taking my happiest day
with him.

There was a blood stain on
my shirt, right over my heart.

Mama will scold me again. This is
my only good shirt and tomorrow
I'm performing at the theater. I'm
going to play the violin.

Everyone was there.
Jacob, Jolly Aaron, Rivka's
grandpa Isaak the Cobbler,
my Aunt Celia and
Aunt Rachel, Big David,
the Blumenthal twins,
and many others. The
theater was packed.

Rivka was in
the second row,
holding the little
dog close.

I was scared that I wouldn't play well.
But I had to prove to Rivka, the dog,
and myself, that I was not a coward.

I began to play. The music grew
and filled the theater. Everything
disappeared—the hall, the seats,
the audience, even the walls.
All that was left was a dazzling
white light. And the music.

But then he appeared.

The **big black bird.**

He spread his wings and let out a loud caw. He looked just like the men in the black uniforms. Was he one of them? I saw his black eyes. He flapped his wings and turned into a knight. His black armor absorbed all the light. There were two black wings on his helmet.

He pulled out a sword
and without a word,
he lunged at me.

But I was ready. My armor sparkled in the light and my sword was strong.

I blocked one blow, then another, and another, and then I attacked.

This was a fight to the end. Only one of us would win. I gave the final thrust. But then I heard a crack. My sword snapped.

Everything disappeared. Mama ran onto the stage and wrapped her arms around me. Isaak the Cobbler patted me on the head, reassuring me: "Don't worry. Tomorrow I'll make you a new bow for your violin."

The theater was silent.
For some reason, Rivka
was rubbing her eyes.

We went home and I fell into bed and slept until noon. When I woke up, Rivka's family was gone. The old cobbler never made me a new bow. People with eyes like dead fish were loading the family's belongings onto a truck.

Aunt Celia came over in the evening and brought the dog. His eye was much better, there was just a little scar on his brow. We stood at the window and looked onto the yard. I pressed him close to my heart. That stain on my shirt never did wash out

Soon it was autumn and the leaves turned golden yellow. There were lots of them on the other side of the wall. Today it was our turn to walk through the gates. The leaves kept falling and falling. We walked down a path of golden leaves. They were so yellow, like the stars on our clothes.

I turned back to look at my
bedroom window. I thought
I heard the wind howling
inside the chimney, but maybe
it was Rivka's little dog, or my
violin crying for its lost bow.
I didn't know. But it didn't
matter to me anymore.

Here, on the
other side of the
wall, the fall was
magnificent.

"Mama, look how yellow
the leaves are, they're as
yellow as my kite."

"Yes, sweetheart."

"Mama, look how smooth
and brown the chestnuts
are. May I pick some?"

"Yes, sweetheart."

"Mama, will we be
there soon?"

"Soon, sweetheart."

"Mama, will Papa be there?
And Rivka?"

Mama didn't answer.
She just turned away.

Soon I grew tired. Mama picked me up
and carried me. We walked on, led by men
in black uniforms and people with dead eyes.

At last, we arrived. There was a commotion. People were swearing, screaming, praying. I was scared and hid in Mama's arms. I curled up into a ball, safe. I knew that nothing could happen to me while I felt her warmth and heard her heart beating. That faint

thump, thump, thump,

which had followed me all my life, now blended with the

thump, thump, thump

of many other hearts. The beating grew faster and faster.

Then something snapped, like the moment my bow broke, and everything went silent.

And so I lay there, curled up in a ball.
It grew dark. The air was cool. I was still
curled up in a little ball with my eyes closed.
I heard the cawing of the crows and the
buzzing of the autumn bees. I wanted to
open my eyes, but my eyelids were so heavy.

Time went by. As
the birds headed south,
they flew in circles
to wish me goodbye.
But I didn't move.

Above me, storms raged
and snow fell. Winter came.
The snowflakes sang me quiet
lullabies. Their cool hands
stroked my back.

Then spring arrived, and the birds
returned. The bees came to visit
me again.

I felt my body change in the sun
and rain. It was becoming smaller,
harder, and smoother, like a pebble.

Days passed, then
months, then years.
I slept.

Then, one day, I felt a tiny,
gentle hand pick me up.

"Grandma!" A little voice
called out. "Look. What a
lovely pebble! It almost seems
alive. Can I take it?"

The woman did not reply. She
picked me up, looked at me closely,
and pressed me to her heart.

I could hear a faint

thump,
     thump,
          thump.

And my stone eyelids opened. The old
woman kissed me and placed me on a grave.

"His place is here, with his family,"
she whispered, and I thought
I could see a tiny scar above
her chapped lips. "Come home,
and I'll tell you their story."

"You mean, he's really alive?"

"Yes, of course. He lives here."
The woman tapped her chest
with her small, strong hand.

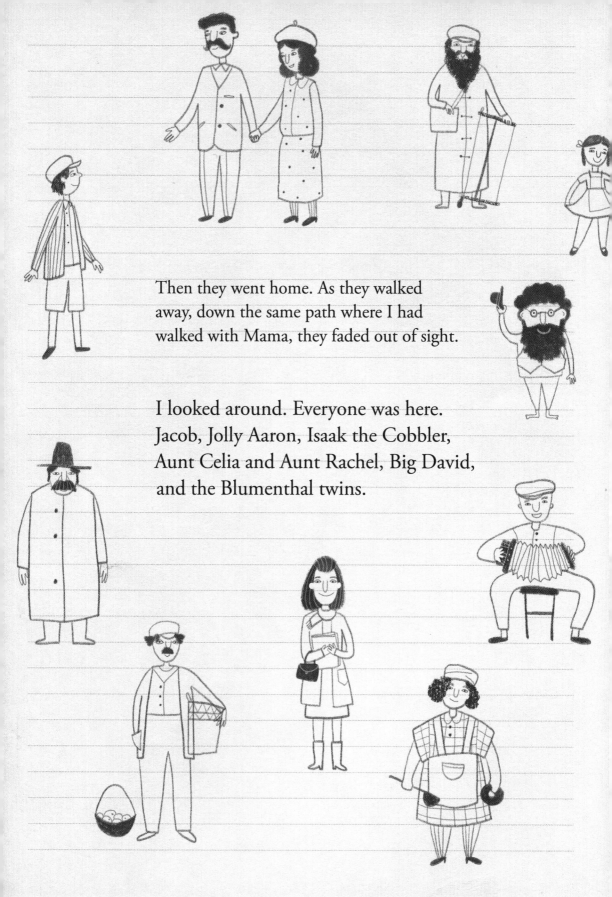

Then they went home. As they walked away, down the same path where I had walked with Mama, they faded out of sight.

I looked around. Everyone was here. Jacob, Jolly Aaron, Isaak the Cobbler, Aunt Celia and Aunt Rachel, Big David, and the Blumenthal twins.

I opened my eyes wider and I
saw Mama and Papa next to me.

And I felt my pebble
body growing warm again.

Me

Leon the
Carpenter

Ana

Papa

Mama

Little
Michael

Rivka

Simeon the
Musician

Adam

Isaak the
Cobbler

Miss Zuzana

Aunt Celia

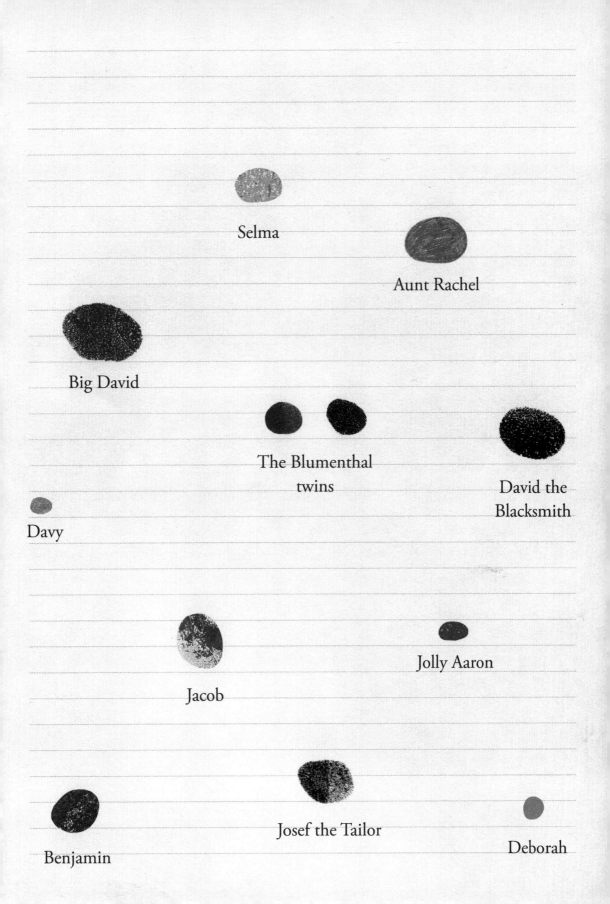

Selma

Aunt Rachel

Big David

The Blumenthal
twins

David the
Blacksmith

Davy

Jacob

Jolly Aaron

Josef the Tailor

Benjamin

Deborah

EPILOGUE

This story takes place in Vilnius in Lithuania, but it could have happened almost anywhere in Europe. World War II was the biggest war in human history. Many people died, but in Europe it was the Jewish people who suffered the most, because the Nazi government wanted to kill them all. This event was called the Holocaust and it lasted more than ten years. During the Holocaust, six million Jews were killed, including one and a half million children.

 All Jews in occupied countries were forced to wear a badge on their clothes, a yellow six-pointed star. This became a symbol of their suffering.

At first, the Jews were separated from the rest of the population. Then the Nazis fenced off entire blocks of the city, closed them and built gates. These districts were called ghettos. It became extremely difficult to live there. The people who lived in the ghetto were forbidden to drive cars or own radios. Life went on, however, and there were art clubs for children, libraries, and even theaters. Most of those who passed through the gates never came back.